For Jenny —A. L.

For Coco: hope your saddle is comfy —R. H.

First published in the United States in 2009 by Chronicle Books LLC.

Text © 2007 by Alison Lester.
Illustrations © 2007 by Roland Harvey.
Originally published in Australia in 2007 by Allen & Unwin under the title *The Circus Pony*.

North American type design by David Habben.
Typeset in Berkeley.
Manufactured in China.

Library of Congress Cataloging-in-Publication Data
Lester, Alison.
[Circus pony]
The circus horse / by Alison Lester ; illustrated by Roland Harvey.
p. cm. — (Horse crazy ; bk. 2)
Summary: In Currawong Creek, Australia, best friends Bonnie and Sam, who share a mutual love of horses, enhance their trick-riding skills when a traveling circus comes to town.
ISBN 978-0-8118-6656-9
[1. Horses—Fiction. 2. Trick riding—Fiction. 3. Circus—Fiction. 4. Friendship—Fiction. 5. Australia—Fiction.] I. Harvey, Roland, ill. II. Title. III. Series.
PZ7.L56284Ci 2009
[Fic]—dc22
2008023014

10 9 8 7 6 5 4 3 2 1

Chronicle Books LLC
680 Second Street, San Francisco, California 94107

www.chroniclekids.com

HORSE crazy

THE CIRCUS HORSE 2

by Alison Lester

illustrated by Roland Harvey

chronicle books · san francisco

ONE HOT AFTERNOON

In summer, Bonnie and Sam always ended the school week with a popsicle at the milk bar.

They loved reading the posters in the window. It was the town noticeboard. If you had guinea pigs to spare or a computer to sell, that's where you'd advertise.

This Friday, the window was full.

"What if we found a *Free to a good home* ad for a beautiful horse?" said Sam. "Wouldn't that be—"

"Look!" Bonnie cut in. "There's a circus coming here in two weeks. Circo's Circus."

"Hey, even better," said Sam, "the fire brigade's running a Talent Night again. Remember when Wally Webster's performing sheep pooed all over the stage?"

"What's the prize?" Bonnie read down the poster. "A video camera for first and a digital camera for second! Third is two hundred photos printed free."

"Wouldn't you love a video camera, Bon?" said Sam. "We could take it with us when we ride up into the mountains. We could film the brumbies. Let's think of something fantastic to do."

"Okay. We've got one week to find out what we're good at."

The Horses of Currawong Creek

Most of the horses in Currawong Creek were looked after by their owners, some better than others. Sam made a point of checking them every day on her way to and from school. Bon often helped her instead of going home to Peppermint Plain on the school bus.

Tricky belonged to Michael Milton, the bossiest boy in the school. Tricky and Michael were the best combination in the pony club games team. They whizzed around barrels and poles so fast that Tricky's black-and-white patches blurred together. But apart from games, Michael ignored Tricky completely. His mother was so sick of nagging him to care for his horse that when Bonnie and Sam offered to do it she quickly said yes.

"Michael doesn't even like you," Bonnie whispered as Tricky rubbed his head against her back. "He just uses you like a motorbike."

Sam turned on the tap to fill the water trough. "Well, Tricky doesn't like him, either. He loves us best, don't you, boy?"

Another horse they checked
every day was Biscuit, a nervous
chestnut mare who belonged to
Wally Webster, the local stock
agent. They gave her a quick rub
and adjusted her fly veil, then
headed for Sam's house. It was
too hot to stay outside.

Sam's little dog Pants came
to meet them, bouncing up and
down on all four paws to make
them laugh.

Bon loved coming home to
Sam's empty house. Sam's dad, Bill, was the
local policeman, so he was never around in the
afternoon. The girls sat on the shady back
veranda, drinking cold lemonade from the fridge
and eating chocolate teddy-bear biscuits.

"Hey, Drover!" Sam called to her father's gray
mare, who was dozing in the shade of the big
eucalyptus tree. Drover pricked one ear, but she
was too lazy to move.

Bonnie and Sam knew a secret that only one other person, Bonnie's Aunty Birdy, knew. Drover was once a brumby, a wild horse, living in the mountains. When she swapped places with Bill's old horse, Birdy had helped the girls teach her to be a policeman's horse. Drover loved the girls, and they rode her nearly every day.

When Bill came home, he reminded Sam that she was going to visit her cousins in the city.

"I'll run you back to Peppermint Plain, Bon, while Sam gets her things together. You can catch up with each other on Sunday."

BORED

On Saturday morning, Bonnie tried to think up an act for the Talent Night while she waited for her mom. They were supposed to be going fishing for crayfish in the big dam. But Woo was a painter, and once she started on a new picture there was no stopping her, no matter what she'd promised.

By late afternoon the painting was far from finished. Bonnie tried everything—begging, pleading, whining, even a mini tantrum—but she might as well have been performing to a fridge.

Finally Bonnie gave up and started flipping
through art books. The afternoon sun and her
mom's painting noises, mixed with music from
the radio, made her sleepy.

Suddenly one picture caught her attention.
It was a painting of a huge gray horse with a
tiny ballerina sitting sideways on its back, her
skirt flying up, and a ringmaster cracking his
whip. Bon read the title: *Equestrienne (At the
Circus Fernando)*.

THE BIG IDEA

When Sam came to Peppermint Plain the next day, Bonnie showed her the picture. "Doesn't it look fantastic? I reckon we could do something like that for the Talent Night. I wonder how we can find out more about it?"

"Let's look it up on your dad's computer," said Sam. "Put in "trick-riding horses" and see what we get."

The girls followed links to find photos of people stepping from one horse to another, galloping "Roman style" on two horses, leaping through fire, and doing the "suicide drag"— hanging upside down between the horse's back legs.

Sam loved the stories about "Poodles" Hanneford, who was famous in the olden days for somersaulting off the back of one horse onto another one following behind.

"Imagine that." She peered into the screen. "It says he was a clown, too. He used to pretend to almost fall off all the time."

Bonnie liked the sound of Rebel Watts. They found pictures of her leaping around her galloping horses like a sequinned fairy.

"It looks so cool. Let's go practice," she said.

The hay shed was the perfect place. They pulled hay bales down from the stack and used them as horses. Bonnie was as nimble as a flea. She could do a somersault in the air. Sam was the opposite.

"You're a POG," said Bonnie, as she tried to help her friend roll forwards. "A Prisoner Of Gravity. But your balance is good. We can be a team."

It wasn't long before Bon could do a backwards somersault off one hay bale onto another, with Sam standing steady to catch her. They had plenty of bruises and scrapes for their efforts.

"That goes with the territory," said Bon. "Rebel broke thirty-seven bones during her career."

"You're pretty good on the flat," said Sam, when they stopped for a breather. "But you need to have a go on something that moves. What about Pedro?"

Bonnie's dad Chester had been bitten by a horse when he was a little boy, and he vowed then that when Peppermint Plain was his it would be horse-free. But he loved cattle, and Peppermint Plain Pedro was his favorite Hereford bull.

Pedro was in the yard beside the hay shed. He was as quiet as an old dog, and let Sam catch him with a piece of baling twine.

Pedro didn't mind when Bonnie vaulted onto his back and stood up straight. She gripped his curly coat with her toes.

"Maybe it's easier on a bull than a horse, Sam. His back is very flat." She swayed as Sam led Pedro into a walk, but kept her balance. He rolled from side to side, his old hooves creaking. "Okay, Sam, I'm going to try a somersault." Bonnie flipped into the air and Sam thought it looked good, but then Pedro exploded into a buck. Bonnie landed on top of Sam and they fell in a heap.

"I think we need a horse," said Bonnie.

The Perfect Pony

The girls had ridden all the horses and ponies of Currawong Creek at some time. Now they made a list, to work out which one would be the best for trick riding.

Drover, Sam's dad's horse, was their favorite. They double-dinked everywhere on her when she wasn't doing police work, but she was too big.

"Let's face it," said Sam, "we're going to fall off a lot, so the less distance we have to fall, the better."

Too tall

Too nervous

Too ugly!

Tarzan was too grumpy. Bonnie's first pony Bella was too small. Her paddock mate, Whale, was way too big. Horrie the racehorse was too nervous. "And too skinny," said Sam. "It would hurt your feet to stand on his bony back."

Chocolate Charm, the dressage horse, was a bit tall, and anyway Cheryl Smythe-Tyght only let the girls ride Choco under her strict super-vision.

Blondie, the palomino, was moody and unpredictable, and Tex, the Appaloosa, was just too ugly.

Too moody   Way too big   Too grumpy

That left Tricky. Bonnie and Sam looked at each other. Tricky would be perfect.

"What about Michael?" said Sam. "He might say no, just to be a meanie."

But—surprise, surprise—at school on Monday, Michael said yes.

"Tell me again what you're going to do," he said, swinging back on his chair with his arms crossed.

Sam took a deep breath. Sometimes Michael was so smug she wanted to punch him in the head.

Bon explained again about the Talent Night, and the trick riding.

"Sure, you can use him." Michael smiled at
the girls as though he was the Pope. "But you
and my stupid horse won't stand a chance.
I'm going to win the Talent Night again with
my violin, just like I did last year."

LEARNING THE CRAFT

"Tricky's back is nearly as flat as Pedro's," Bon said as they double-dinked along Currawong Creek, looking for a sandy flat to practice on.

"Mmmn." Sam couldn't forget Michael's smirk when they told him their plan. "I hope he doesn't buck you off."

But Tricky was perfect. With Bonnie on his back he trotted in a circle, keeping an even rhythm and avoiding any small dips in the sand.

"It's as though he wants to make it easy for you," Sam called from the center of the circle.

"That's what it feels like." Bonnie balanced carefully, arms held wide, and smiled into the evening sun. "He's loving it."

After a little while, Sam unclipped the long rein from Tricky's headstall and let the pony trot freely. He continued his perfect circles. Bonnie began to experiment, first bending backward until her hands were resting on Tricky's rump, then kicking up to hold a handstand for a few seconds, then somersaulting onto the ground behind him.

"Woo hoo!" Sam ran over to help her friend up. "You're a natural, Bon."

Every after-
noon after school,
Bonnie and Sam
took Tricky down to
Currawong Creek and practiced their trick riding. Bonnie was the star now, and she loved it.
Usually Sam was the best at riding.

Bonnie quickly learned how to use the pony's
rhythm to vault on and off his back while he
trotted, and she could catch a beach ball Sam
threw to her at the same time. She taught Sam
how to swing up too. They developed that into
an act where Bonnie climbed onto Sam's shoulders and stood, arms outstretched, as Tricky
cantered around and around.

By Friday afternoon they had perfected
enough tricks for a ten-minute performance, the
maximum time allowed at the Talent Night. They
had paid the $15 fee and filled in the entry form.
They were ready for Saturday night!

Sam sat on a log and watched Bonnie stand
on her hands as Tricky trotted past the creek.
Evening shadows made stripes across the clearing,
flashing light and dark across Tricky's back. Pants
ran behind him, yipping in time to his trot.

We're going to win this, Sam thought,
imagining herself dressed in
the ringmaster costume from
the dress-up box, and Bonnie
in her tutu. Perhaps Pants could
be part of the show too, with
a ruffle around
her collar.

BROKEN DREAMS

Sam broke out of her daydream when Michael Milton plonked down beside her.

"Great stuff. Really impressive."

Sam could hardly believe her ears. "Thanks, Michael. He's an excellent pony."

"Yes, it's a pity you've gone to all this trouble for nothing." Michael smirked his nastiest grin, yawned extravagantly, and stretched his legs. "Such a shame they're not allowing any animal acts this year. No exceptions. After the poo problem last year, the hall committee made it a condition."

"But we can do it outside," Sam stammered. "And they've taken our entry money."

"No," said Michael. "They won't let you perform. I heard Mother talking on the phone." He stood up and yawned again. "Anyway, I'd better go and practise my violin. She'll kill me if I don't win again."

As he scuttled away through the shadows,
Sam looked across at her clever friend, balancing on Tricky like a bird. He knew all along,
she thought. The stinker knew they wouldn't be
allowed to perform. That's why he'd been smirking when he said they could use Tricky.

"Bonnie!" she shouted. "Stop! I've got to tell
you something."

It was true. When the girls asked Stumpy
Shelton, captain of the fire department, he said
Michael was right and gave them their money
back. "I'm sorry, girls, but it's the insurance.
The stupid insurance."

Sam could feel tears welling up in her eyes.
Bonnie looked as though she might start howl-
ing too, so Sam put her arm around her.

"Thanks anyway, Mr Shelton," she mumbled.
"I know it's not your fault."

Bonnie's mom, Woo, was always willing to
fight stupid official decisions, but even she could

see that arguing wouldn't do any good this time.

"Let's boycott the Talent Night," she suggested. "If they won't let my girls perform, I don't want to go."

"Thanks, Mom," said Bonnie. "But I don't want to be a bad sport. And it was really funny last year, wasn't it, Sam? Even if Michael was a pain."

"Here's an idea," said Woo. "Let's go to the talent show tomorrow, then on Sunday evening we can have a picnic down on the creek, with a special performance of your act, just for our families."

Bonnie jumped up with a whoop. "Good on you, Mom! That would be fantastic."

Sam didn't feel sad any more. "Come on, Bon. Let's get our costumes organized." As long as they could perform for the people who loved them, that was all that mattered.

First Prize

Everybody at the Talent Night had heard about Bonnie and Sam's disappointment. The girls lost count of how many people wished them well.

"It's like we're heroes or something," Sam murmured to Bonnie.

"That's because we came," said Bon. "If we'd stayed away, we'd have looked like wimps."

Michael played his violin perfectly, and for a while it looked as though he would win.

"It wouldn't be fair if he had two video cameras," Bon whispered, and Sam felt a nasty stab of jealousy.

But the last act of the night stole the show. Shy Mr. Briggs the butcher, and his little girl, Tamsin, sang "You Are My Sunshine" together, dancing and holding up cardboard shapes of sunshine, clouds, and rain. They were so sweet that the applause lasted nearly five minutes, making them clear winners.

The Morgan family came second with their version of "Do-Re-Mi" from *The Sound of Music*. Mrs. Morgan had sewn costumes for them out of curtain material, and the audience clapped for her hard work as much as for her family's terrible singing.

Michael came third, and he wasn't happy. "What good is free photo processing when I haven't got a camera?" Bonnie overheard him grumbling. "You'll have to buy me one, Mother."

The Circus Comes to Town

Thunderclouds rolled in on Sunday, so the picnic and trick-riding show had to be postponed until the next weekend. By Monday, the sun was out again and the whole town looked washed clean.

When Bonnie and Sam checked the horses, as usual, on the way home from school, they heard a loud hammering coming from the soccer ground. An enormous tent was going up.

"It's the circus! I'd forgotten all about it!" Bonnie pulled Sam's arm and started running. "Let's check it out."

Caravans and trucks were parked around the edge of the oval with the big tent in the middle. The girls squeezed between two vans and stared at the busy scene. There was so much going on that nobody noticed them. People were hammering in huge tent pegs, putting up temporary pens, attaching annexes to caravans. Everyone was running.

Bonnie read aloud some of the advertising painted on the vans. "Old McDonald's Clever Cows; The Flying Pans; Cisco the Clown; Samson, the Biggest Horse in Australia; Doctor Dog and his Tailwaggers; Bomberino the Fire-Eater; Miguel's Performing Horses and La Bella Donna, the Trick Rider." Bonnie gave a little squeal. "It's gonna be fantastic! Lets go and find the horses."

CIRCUS HORSES

"What are you kids doing?" A skinny man in a black cowboy hat appeared in front of them. "You can't just wander around here."

Sam stood her ground. "Anyone can be here. It's the soccer arena."

The man smiled and smoothed his thin mustache. "Pardon me, señoritas." He pulled a folded paper from the back pocket of his dirty jeans, and waved it in the air. "This permit from the council says we can use this ground exclusively for the next week. Circo's Circus, which means me, Mr. Circo, can tell anybody to get out." He pushed the paper under Sam's nose and bowed. "And I am telling you to get out. Vamoose! On your way, ladies. Come back on Friday night for the show."

Bonnie and Sam headed for the main gate, walking backward sometimes to see as much as they could. Mr. Circo watched them all the way.

"He's making sure we don't duck around behind a truck," said Sam, waving to him. "But I know how to get in the back of the grandstand. We can hide up high and watch from there."

The girls sat together on the very top step of the grandstand. It was perfect. They could see the whole arena with all the horses. Trucks and caravans were parked all around, to screen it from the road.

"Wow! That horse is as big as a house," Bon pointed. "He'd make Whale look like a pony. It must be Samson."

They watched a slim figure lead a black pony into the arena and start to lunge him in a circle.

"That must be Bella Donna." Sam squinted to see the girl's face. "She doesn't look much older than us."

Now the pony was circling smoothly. The girl unclipped the lunging rein, ran beside him and vaulted onto his back.

"Look! She's got a special saddle thing, Bonnie. That would make it so much easier. There's a handle on the pommel and loops for your feet."

Bonnie couldn't take her eyes off the rider. "I'd love to talk to her, but they don't seem very friendly."

THE CIRCUS GIRL

On Tuesday after school, Bonnie and Sam took Tricky down to the creek again.

"The Talent Night's over, losers," sneered Michael. "Why are you still practicing?"

The girls just ignored him. Bonnie had taught Pants how to run in front of Tricky, holding his lead rein. They wanted to see if Tricky would run in circles after Pants without the rein.

Sam put an old pony pad on Tricky, with a breastplate, and it made things much easier for Bonnie. She was trying to do the suicide drag, lying right back on Tricky's rump, when he snorted and pulled up suddenly.

"What the . . . ?" Bonnie sat up and her heart jumped. On the other side of the creek was the girl from the circus, on her black pony. Her reins were loose and the pony seemed to be waiting for a signal.

"Come over!" Bonnie shouted. "It's not deep."

The black pony picked his way across Currawong Creek as delicately as a ballet dancer, and the girl sat on his back like a princess.

Bonnie slid off Tricky and stepped forward.

"Hi, you must be Bella Donna. I'm Bonnie," she said.

Sam poked a finger to her chest. "And I'm Sam."

37

The beautiful dark-eyed girl smiled. "Actually, I'm just Bella, Bella Salvador. The Donna part is just for show." She slid off her gleaming pony and patted his neck. "And this is Jet. What about you two? You look like you're trick riders too."

"Not proper trick riders," Bon said. "We're just learning."

She jumped aside as Tricky barged up to Jet, ears pricked, and the two ponies sniffed each other. The tension broke with a squeal and a toss of heads.

Sam pulled Tricky away. "Sorry. He has terrible manners. He thinks he's the star."

"He could be," Bella said. "He's beautiful."

Bonnie and Sam told her about the Talent Night and their squashed dreams.

"Yesterday, we saw your special saddle, so we were experimenting with Sam's old pony pad," Bonnie explained. "Until now I've been doing it all bareback."

Bella ran her hand along Tricky's back. "I couldn't do what you've been doing, bareback. But I can show you some of my tricks."

The next two hours went faster than any time Bonnie had ever known, as Bella shared her skills. When it was time to go, Sam invited Bella to her house after school the next day. "We'll meet here at four o'clock, okay?"

MORE ABOUT
THE CIRCUS

At school the next day, everybody was talking about the circus!

"They don't even have lions and elephants," scoffed Michael Milton.

Bonnie and Sam didn't tell a soul about meeting Bella Donna, but they defended the circus fiercely.

"It's cruel to make wild animals perform," Bonnie told the class, "so they use domestic animals, like cows and dogs and horses."

CIRCO'S
CIRCUS
⭐ Old McDonald's CLEVER COWS !!
⭐ the FLYING PAMS !
⭐ CISCO the CLOWN !!
⭐ SAMPSON, the BIGGEST HORSE in AUSTRALIA !!
⭐ DOCTOR DOG & his TAILWAGGERS !!
⭐ BELLA DONNA, the TRICK RIDER !!
⭐ BOMBERINO, the FIRE-EATER !!
⭐ MIGUEL'S PERFORMING HORSES !!

CURRAWONG CREEK FOOTBALL OVAL
THIS WEEK ONLY!

Bella arrived after school, and the three girls talked for hours about their different lives. It turned out that Bella's family lived on a farm in Queensland when the circus wasn't touring.

"Nanna and Pop look after things while we're away," she said.

Bella had twin six-year-old brothers who dressed up as baby pandas in the circus. "Everybody has something to do," she explained. "Even when I was a baby, Dad made me part of the show. That's how it is in a circus."

"My dad told me that when he was little the circus kids used to go to Currawong Creek school while they were in town," said Sam.

"Yep, that's right," Bella nodded. "My dad hated it." She rubbed Pants's tummy with her foot. "Our moms and dads had a rotten time, always changing schools. So now we have our own traveling school, with a teacher and a special trailer. And we do correspondence work on the Internet."

THE ACCIDENT

When Bella came to the creek on Thursday, she had put the trick-riding saddle on Jet, so she could show the girls her fancy tricks.

Jet's glossy coat shimmered as he circled neatly, neck arched. When Bella finished her full routine, Bonnie and Sam clapped and hooted like lunatics.

"Okay." Bella swung off her pony. "Now it's your turn."

It was as though Tricky wanted to impress Jet. He didn't put a foot wrong, and Bonnie danced on his back like a fairy. Bella couldn't get over how well Bonnie balanced bareback.

Then Bella sat on Tricky, and he trotted forward. "Whoo! He feels so different from Jet!" she called, and jumped to her feet in one fluid movement. But, that very moment, Tricky stumbled on a patch of heavy sand and sent Bella flying through the air. She looked so graceful that Bonnie and Sam started to clap, but the scream she let out as she hit the ground silenced them.

"Oooh! My ankle!" she cried, holding her foot. "I think it's broken!" She huddled over, making squeaky crying noises.

"Let me see." Sam patted Bella's shoulder.

"I must have landed on something hard. Sorry. I never cry. Really. But this hurts."

Bella's ankle was as fat as a piglet.

"It needs ice," Sam said. "I'll race up to the house and get some."

"Mom and Dad will be furious," Bella sniffed as Bonnie held a packet of frozen peas against her ankle. "My act is always the finale. Mr C. will probably give Dad the sack if I can't do it."

"Is your dad Miguel?" Sam asked, still puffing from her run.

"Yep, Miguel's Performing Horses," Bella replied. "But he hurt his back last year and hasn't been able to ride since. Mr. Circo has been threatening to get a new horse master for months. If it wasn't for me and the twins, he would have."

"I thought he looked like a rat," said Sam. "Let me bandage your ankle. I don't think it's broken, just badly sprained." Sam knew a lot about first aid from her dad.

"What am I going to do?" wailed Bella. "I can't even stand up. There's no way it's going to be better by tomorrow night."

"Maybe Bonnie can fill in for you," Sam suggested.

"That's it!" For the first time since her fall, Bella smiled. "You could easily do it, Bonnie. Look at us, we're nearly the same size and shape. With my costume and makeup on, nobody will be able to tell the difference."

Bonnie felt a shiver of excitement. A real circus rider!

"Come on," Bella begged her. "Please say you'll at least try. Hop on Jet now and see how you do."

But when Bonnie hopped on Jet, he wouldn't go at all. He laid his ears back flat against his head, so he looked like a black snake, and refused to move.

All the girls' cajoling and bossing made no difference. Even when Bonnie leaned forward and whispered her special horse talk in his ear, Jet wouldn't budge. He only went for one rider, and that was Bella.

"You're a pig, Jet," Bella shouted at him, crying tears of frustration. "I hate you!"

"I saw a horse do this at the Melbourne Cup one year," Sam said, trying to calm Bella. "I was watching it on TV and this horse just stopped on the way to the starting stalls and wouldn't budge for anyone. You can't make a horse do something it doesn't want to do."

"I bet it didn't get much dinner that night," Bon laughed, and then added, as a joke, "I could always do the performance on Tricky. If we painted his legs black and put a big saddlecloth on him to cover his white bits, most people wouldn't know the difference."

Bella shook both fists in the air. "You're a genius, Bonnie," she shouted. "Put my saddle on Tricky right away and I'll teach you my routine."

Bonnie wasn't nearly as slick as Bella, but she could do everything except the grand finale. She was supposed to do a somersault in the air and land on Tricky's back.

Tricky had to slow down at exactly the right time, but after getting so good at trotting steadily he didn't want to slow down. Each time, Bonnie landed on the ground instead of on his back.

"It will just have to do," Bella said. "Most people will think that's what's supposed to happen anyway."

Bonnie and Sam helped her onto Jet's back, then swung onto Tricky.

"What about your mom?" Bonnie asked. "She's got to notice you can't walk."

Bella shifted in the saddle. "Tonight I'll pretend I have only one leg."

Sam smiled. It was the kind of crazy thing she and Bonnie would do. Her dad would just roll his eyes and say, "What next?"

"Then tomorrow I'll ask Mom if I can have my day in bed. She lets us have one day in bed each term."

Mrs. Salvador sounded like a very cool mom.

"I'll have to tell the twins. They love secrets. I'll tell them to bring Jet to your house at six o'clock. I'll disappear, so Mom thinks I'm getting ready. You can swap Tricky for Jet and come back with the boys."

"Mighty fine plan," Sam laughed. "I'll put Jet in the paddock with Drover."

The three girls smacked hands in a high five, then turned their horses toward home.

SECRETS

"What do you think?" Sam held up a crimson satin tablecloth with aqua tassels and "Greetings from Hervey Bay" printed in one corner. "This should cover most of Tricky's white bits."

"Cool," said Bon. "Help me black out the rest."

The girls brushed Tricky until he shone and braided his mane and tail.

Then Sam painted Bon's face in the way Bella had suggested: white with red cheeks, like a marionette.

When Bella's brothers came through the garden they were so alike that the girls couldn't help laughing. They were tiny, with short black hair and big brown eyes.

"They look like pandas even without their costumes," Sam whispered.

"Hi, boys. I'm Sam and this is Bonnie. She's going to fill in for Bella tonight."

Alphonso and Augustin were extremely serious about the operation. One of them handed Bonnie a bulging plastic bag. "This is her costume. She said to make sure you put the tights on first or it won't work."

"We've got to go on at seven-fifteen, so you have to hurry," said the other.

Sam draped the tablecloth over Tricky's back, and lowered Bella's trick-riding saddle onto it.

"Make sure you do the girth up tight," said Alphonso or Augustin, "or she'll go flying."

UNDER THE BIG TOP

Sam sat between her dad and Bon's parents, watching the little boys in their panda suits. They teased the clown and ringmaster, pushing them from behind, then hid behind barrels and balls. The crowd roared with laughter.

"Where's Bon?" Woo asked again. "It's not like her to miss the action."

"She's helping Bella. You know, the circus girl we met." Sam's face went red whenever she told a fib, so she was glad the lights were dim.

They watched the Flying Pans whizz through the air above them, laughed until they wept at the clever cows and dogs, shrieked in fear for Bomberino the Fire-Eater, and gasped at Samson, the Biggest Horse in Australia.

Sam could see that Bella's father had a sore back by the way he walked, but he still looked dignified. The horses watched him all the time,

as though they were determined to do their very best. Sam's dad noticed it too.

"He's a real horseman," he nudged Sam. "See how the horses love him."

They clapped until their hands were sore when ten tiny ponies trotted nose-to-tail underneath the giant Samson, who nodded his head as each one passed.

"Thank you, ladies and gentlemens, girls and boys!" Mr. Circo shouted, as Miguel and his horses left the big top. "And now for our final act, our world-class equestrienne, La Bella Donna!"

THE BIG MOMENT

Sam felt sick as Tricky entered the arena with Bonnie sitting bravely on his back. He looked frightened, ready to shy at anything. What if he wouldn't go? But Bon leaned forward, whispered in his ear, and his expression changed.

Music filled the tent, and Tricky began to circle over the sawdust. Bonnie sat still at first, arms stretched wide, and the audience hushed.

She looks like the real deal, thought Sam.

Mr. Circo didn't seem to have noticed anything wrong. He was standing alone in the middle of the ring, watching the audience.

Suddenly Bonnie jumped to her feet and began bouncing from Tricky onto the ground and up again, standing on her hands, spinning, twisting, and hanging her head between his back legs. Her movements were so quick in the glittering golden costume that it was hard to believe a human could move so lightly and so fast.

Tricky was perfect, his neck arched, his black legs crisscrossing neatly over the sawdust. Bonnie spun above him like a golden fairy, working through Bella's tricks.

As she slowed for the finale, Mr. Circo boomed into the microphone. "And now, La Bella Donna will zomersault and land once more on ze pony's back."

The music softened and he lowered his voice dramatically. "I remind you, ladies and gentle-mens, that ze zomersault takes time, and in zat time ze pony moves. Ozer riders 'ave zomer-saulted onto anozer 'orse, ozer riders have zom-ersaulted onto ze ground, but none but La Bella Donna has zomersaulted onto ze same 'orse. It takes a great understanding between 'orse and rider to achieve zis feat! Ladies and gentlemens, I present ze Zuper Zomersault!"

Sam held her breath. What was Bonnie going to do? Everyone was waiting for a trick she'd never managed before.

Bonnie leaned forward again to whisper in Tricky's ear, and the crowd murmured. It seemed as if the pony was listening to her. But when she flung herself into the air, it was clear that he hadn't slowed enough for her to land properly. She landed way back on his rump, slipped, twisted, then hung back with her head between Tricky's hind legs in a suicide drag.

The crowd gasped then applauded as Bonnie pulled herself back onto the pony. Almost immediately she fell sideways, and Sam screamed, like the rest of the audience.

As Bonnie turned that near-fall into another move, Sam realized she was playing the clown, like Poodles Hanneford. If she couldn't do the somersault, she was going to give them a laugh. But when Sam looked at Mr. Circo's face, he wasn't laughing.

The Rescue

Sam squeezed past Woo who was too mesmerised by La Bella Donna to notice. She hurried out of the tent and stood in the dark, whistling, the same long whistle, over and over. Laughter and applause from inside the big top told her that Bon was still clowning.

Suddenly a white shape rushed out of the dark. "Pants!" She hugged her dog and got a wet lick in return. "You little beauty!"

Sam and Pants wriggled under the seats to the front row. "Pants, I need you to slow Tricky down. Here, you scruffy girl," she said, pulling the lime-green scrunchy out of her hair and putting it around Pants's neck. "Now you look like a circus dog." She kissed Pants on the nose, then put her down. "Go Pants! Lead Tricky!"

The crowd roared even louder when the little dog entered the ring and ran proudly in front of

Tricky. Tricky slowed to follow Pants. Mr. Circo looked as though he was going to explode.

Bon saw Pants, too, and knew this was her only chance. She gathered her strength, and then twisted up and backward, spinning, spinning. . . and landed on Tricky's back.

The crowd went crazy. Bonnie had done the Super Somersault. She stood up straight, arms held high, as Tricky cantered around the ring, with wave after wave of applause washing over her golden sequinned suit.

FOUND OUT

When Sam burst into the dressing tent, all she could see in the glare was Bonnie, Bella, and Tricky. "You did it!" she screamed. "You were fantastic! Nobody could tell the difference!"

"I could tell the difference." Suddenly Sam realised that Bella's parents were there. Mrs. Salvador was tiny and dark, like Bella. "I knew straight away that it wasn't my daughter," she said.

"And I knew it was *my* daughter," said a voice behind them. Woo pushed past Sam, followed by Bon's dad, and Bill Cooper. "I think you kids better tell us what's going on."

After that it turned into a party. The adults were secretly proud of their clever kids.

Mr. Circo didn't know whether to shout with anger or happiness. "And what if your friend hadn't been a natural rider?" he asked Bella. "What then?" He smoothed his mustache, sighed loudly and looked upward. "You must never go riding on ponies again. You're too important for the circus. Understand?"

He ruffled Bella's hair and hugged Mrs. Salvador. "But maybe, Miguel," he said to Bella's dad, "maybe we will have to work some of Bonnie's clown act into the show."

THE REAL FINALE

On Saturday, there was a picnic at Bonnie and Sam's practice spot beside Currawong Creek. Aunty Birdy came, and Janice and Bob from the newsstand, and Cheryl Smythe-Tyght. Bella's parents and little brothers and Mr. Circo and some other circus families were there too.

Tricky was black-and-white again. Pants ran in front of Tricky with a purple ruffle around her neck, looking very important.

Bonnie and Sam started their performance with simple tricks, and the applause got louder after each move. When Bonnie finally stood on Sam's shoulders and double-somersaulted backward onto the ground, everyone went crazy. Even Mr. Circo was impressed.

As the sky turned pink then faded to purple, the families sat on rugs in the sandy clearing and shared a feast. Sam's dad and Miguel

chatted over the barbeque sausages, and realized they had sat together in school, thirty years ago.

"I never forgot you," said Miguel. "You helped me with long division."

The next day, as the circus was leaving, Bonnie and Sam rode beside Bella's caravan to the outskirts of town, double-dinking on Tricky.

"She'll always be our friend," said Bonnie as the circus cavalcade disappeared down the road. "Won't she?"

"That's right," said Sam, kicking Tricky into a canter. "We are the Tricky Trio. The girls who tricked a town."

The girls put Tricky back in his paddock, and rewarded him with carrots for his good work. Michael Milton raced up and skidded to a stop on his new mountain bike.

"Did ya go to the circus?" He sat back and spun his front wheel. "That Bella Donna on Jet was fantastic. Not like you and my stupid horse."

Bonnie and Sam laughed so hard that they fell over.

Tricky raced around the paddock, bucking and farting, and Pants ran after him, barking.

"What's so funny?" asked Michael.